MICHAEL DAHL PRESENTS
SUPER FUNNY
JOKE BOOKS

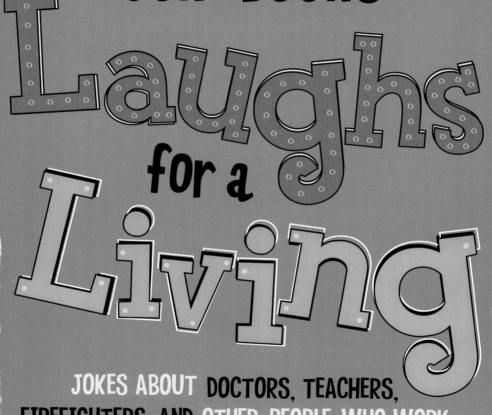

Laughs for a **Living**

JOKES ABOUT DOCTORS, TEACHERS,
FIREFIGHTERS, AND OTHER PEOPLE WHO WORK

PICTURE WINDOW BOOKS
a capstone imprint

MICHAEL DAHL PRESENTS SUPER FUNNY JOKE BOOKS

are published by Picture Window Books
a Capstone Imprint
151 Good Counsel Drive, P.O. Box 669
Mankato, Minnesota 56002
www.capstonepub.com

Doctor, Doctor, Under Arrest, and *Three-Alarm Jokes* were previously published
by Picture Window Books copyright, © 2004
Wacky Workers and *What's Up, Doc?* were previously published
by Picture Window Books, copyright © 2006

Library of Congress Cataloging-in-Publication data
is available on the Library of Congress website.
ISBN: 978-1-4048-5771-1 (library binding)
ISBN: 978-1-4048-6368-2 (paperback)

Art Director: KAY FRASER
Designer: EMILY HARRIS
Production Specialist: JANE KLENK

TABLE OF CONTENTS

UNDERCOVER LAUGHS:
POLICE JOKES

What do you call a flying police officer?

A helicopper.

What did the thief say when he robbed the glue factory?

"This is a stickup!"

What do you call a freezing police officer?

A copsicle.

What did the picture say when the cop sent it to jail by mistake?

"I've been framed!"

Officer: Sir, please call your dog. He's chasing a man on a bicycle.

Dog Owner: That must be somebody else's dog. Mine can't ride a bicycle.

What is a robber's favorite dinner?

Takeout.

Why did the police officer stay in bed all day?

He was an undercover cop.

Why did the police arrest the baseball player?

Because he stole third base.

Why did the burglar take a shower?

He wanted to make a clean getaway.

What do traffic cops have in their sandwiches?

Traffic jam.

Why was the bird arrested by the police?

Because it was a robin.

Why did the police look inside the cement mixer?

They were looking for hardened criminals.

What kind of robber has the strongest arms?

A shoplifter.

Why did the police officer arrest the suspenders?

Because they held up a pair of pants.

WHY DID THE POLICE OFFICER ARREST THE KITTENS?

BECAUSE OF THE KITTY LITTER.

RED-HOT LAUGHS:

FIREFIGHTER JOKES

Why do firefighters keep dogs in their stations?

To help them find the fire hydrants.

What was the firefighter's favorite song?

Ring of Fire.

What kind of crackers do firefighters put in their soup?

Firecrackers!

Bang! POP! POW!

Why did the firefighter wear stilts to work?

He wanted a raise.

What's the difference between a firefighter and her dog?

A firefighter wears a full suit, but the dog only pants.

Why was the firefighter stressed out?

He was always alarmed.

Why did the firefighter bring his ladder to the library?

He heard the library had a lot of stories.

Why do firefighters slide down the pole?

Because they can't slide up!

What's a firefighter's favorite dessert?

Apple crisp.

What kind of car does a firefighter drive?

A Blazer.

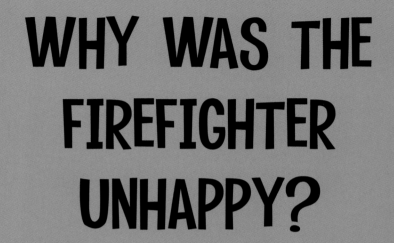

WHY WAS THE FIREFIGHTER UNHAPPY?

EVERY TIME HE WORKED, HE GOT FIRED.

What do you call a contest between two firefighters?

A match.

Firefighter 1: Why is it so hot in here?

Firefighter 2: Because we always have to take the heat when something goes wrong.

Why was the fire chief annoyed?

Because he was always asked burning questions.

What happened to the firefighter who kept going back to college?

He got third-degree burnout.

Man: My house is on fire!

Firefighter: How do I get there?

Man: Drive your big red truck!

HOW DO FIREFIGHTERS STAY SO WARM AT NIGHT?

THEY ALWAYS SLEEP BETWEEN FIRES.

LAUGHTER IS THE BEST MEDICINE:

DOCTOR JOKES

Patient: Doctor, my brother thinks he's invisible!

Doctor: Tell him I can't see him now.

Patient: Doctor, I feel like a window.

Doctor: Where's the pane?

Patient: Doctor, can you help me? I'm a burglar.

Doctor: Have you taken anything for it?

Patient: Doctor, I feel run down.

Doctor: Be more careful crossing the street!

Patient: Doctor, will this lotion clear up the red spots on my arm?

Doctor: I never make rash promises.

Patient: Doctor, can you help me out?

Doctor: Yes, which way did you come in?

Patient: Doctor, I've got gas.

Doctor: Good. Go fill up my car.

Patient: Doctor, everyone disagrees with me.

Doctor: No they don't!

Patient: Doctor, I think I'm turning into a needle.

Doctor: I see your point.

Patient: Doctor, I think I'm a cashew!

Doctor: You must be nuts!

Patient: Doctor, I have this feeling I'm getting smaller and smaller.

Doctor: Don't worry. You'll just have to be a little patient.

Patient: Doctor, I snore so loudly I keep waking myself up.

Doctor: Then sleep in another room.

Patient: Doctor, everyone thinks I'm a liar.

Doctor: I find that hard to believe.

Patient: Doctor, I think I'm losing my memory!

Doctor: When did this happen?

Patient: When did what happen?

Patient: Doctor, my mom thinks she's a deck of cards.

Doctor: I'll deal with her later.

Patient: Doctor, I feel like a bridge!

Doctor: Well, what's come over you?

Patient: Doctor, what did the X-ray of my head show?

Doctor: Absolutely nothing.

Patient: Doctor, I keep hearing a ringing in my ears.

Doctor: Then answer the phone!

PATIENT: DOCTOR, I FEEL LIKE A PAIR OF CURTAINS!

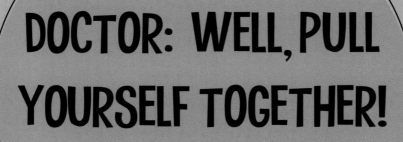

DOCTOR: WELL, PULL YOURSELF TOGETHER!

Patient: Doctor, my sister thinks she's a pony!

Doctor: She does sound a little horse.

Patient: Doctor, I feel like a blueberry.

Doctor: Sounds like you're in a jam.

34

Patient: Doctor, my little brother fell down the stairs!

Doctor: Don't worry. I'll get to the bottom of it.

Nurse: Doctor, are you finished operating on this patient?

Doctor: Yes. I've had quite enough out of him!

Patient: Doctor, I feel flushed!

Doctor: Then don't sit
on the toilet!

Patient: Doctor, I think I have too
much iron in my diet.

Doctor: Then stop chewing your nails.

Patient: Doctor, I feel like a hamburger.

Doctor: So do I. Order two of them.

Patient: Doctor, my sister swallowed a spoon!

Doctor: Tell her to sit still and not stir.

Patient: Doctor, sometimes my nose swells up like a doorknob.

Doctor: You need to get a grip.

37

Why did the comedian go to the doctor?

He was feeling a little funny.

Patient: Doctor, my nose keeps running.

Doctor: Wait for it to get tired. You'll be able to catch it.

Doctor: Nurse, how is that little boy who swallowed the ten quarters doing?

Nurse: No change yet.

Patient: Doctor, I need glasses.

Salesperson: You sure do! This is a shoe store.

What did one tonsil say to the other?

Get dressed. The doctor is taking us out tonight!

Patient: Doctor, I feel like a spider.

Doctor: Don't worry. You've just caught a bug.

Patient: Doctor, my sister just swallowed my pencil.

Doctor: Then use a pen.

Patient: Doctor, I think I'm an electric eel.

Doctor: How shocking!

Patient: Doctor, I feel like two different people.

Doctor: I'll see you one at a time.

Patient: Doctor, I feel like a rubber band.

Doctor: I think you're stretching things.

Patient: Doctor, I think I'm turning into a thumbtack.

Doctor: I see your point!

Patient: Doctor, I keep seeing a big fly buzzing around my head.

Doctor: It's just a bug going around.

Patient: Doctor, my father keeps acting like a goat!

Doctor: How long has he been this way?

Patient: Ever since he was a kid.

WACKY WORKERS:

WAITERS, DENTISTS, TEACHERS, AND MORE

Why did the carpenter stop making wooden cars?

They wooden go.

What are a plumber's favorite shoes?

Clogs.

Why did the dentist have a bad date with the manicurist?

Because they fought tooth and nail!

Why did the engineer go to locomotive school?

He needed training.

Customer: Waiter, do you serve crabs here?

Waiter: We serve everybody.

Why was the mail carrier so soggy?

She had postage dew.

US MAIL

Why did the reporter order an ice-cream cone?

He wanted to get the scoop.

Why was the mattress salesman fired?

He was caught lying on the job.

Customer: Waiter, can I order the same thing I had yesterday?

Waiter: Of course not! You ate it already.

What job has its ups and downs?

A roller-coaster operator.

Who gets the most respect in a kindergarten class?

The teacher. All her students look up to her.

Whose job is always looking up?

An astronomer.

Customer: Waiter, can I eat anything on the menu?

Waiter: No. You'll have to eat it on a plate.

Why didn't the butcher sell lunch meat?

He thought it was a bunch of bologna.

What did one real-estate agent say to another real-estate agent?

"House it going?"

Customer: Waiter, this soup tastes funny.

Waiter: Then why aren't you laughing?

Why did the plumber fall asleep at work?

His job was draining.

Why was the baker so rich?

She had a lot of dough.

Who always starts her job by stopping?

A bus driver.

Why did the accountant have sore feet?

He was working on income tacks.

What does the dentist of the year get?

A little plaque.

Customer: Waiter, there's a twig in my soup!

Waiter: Yes. Our restaurant has branches everywhere.

Where do math teachers eat?

At the lunch counter.

What nail doesn't a carpenter like to hit?

His fingernail.

How did the human cannonball lose his job?

He was fired.

What do you call a happy cowboy?

A jolly rancher.

CUSTOMER:

WAITER, THERE'S A BEE IN MY ALPHABET SOUP!

WAITER:

AND I'M SURE THERE'S AN A, C, AND ALL THE OTHER LETTERS, TOO.

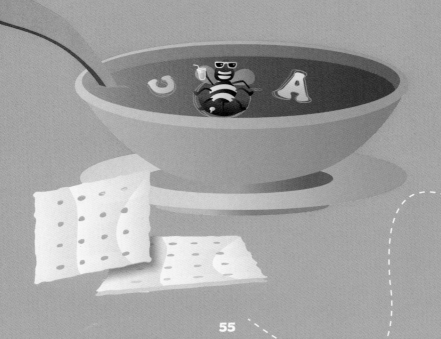

Customer: Waitress, do you have chicken legs?

Waitress: No. I've always walked like this.

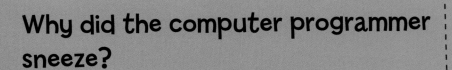

Why did the computer programmer sneeze?

He had a virus.

Why did the painter get so hot?

He kept putting on another coat.

Customer: Waiter, there's an insect in the butter!

Waiter: Yes. We call that a butterfly.

Why did the king go to the dentist?

To get a crown.

What do you call someone who makes faces all day?

A clock maker.

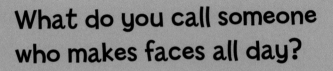

What did the electrician drive to work?

A Volts wagon.

Why did the lazy kid work at the shoe store?

She was a loafer.

What do lawyers wear to court?

Lawsuits.

Why did the tree go to the dentist?

To get a root canal.

What person always falls down on the job?

A paratrooper.

Customer: Waiter, do you have any lobster tails?

Waiter: Yes, we do. Once upon a time, there was a little lobster . . .

What time do you go to the dentist?

Tooth-hurty.

Why was the lawyer in and out of the courtroom so fast?

She had a briefcase.

What kind of car does a farmer drive?

A cornvertible.

WHY DID THE GRAVEDIGGER QUIT HIS JOB?

HE WAS TIRED OF THE HOLE BUSINESS.

PUNCHING A CLOCK:

Quick One-liners and Puns

Jack wanted to be a barber, but he just couldn't cut it.

Brian tried to work in a muffler factory, but that job was exhausting.

Julie tried to be a tailor, but she just wasn't suited for it.

The personal trainer had to quit her job because it wasn't working out.

Joe worked as a lumberjack, but he couldn't hack it. His boss gave him the axe.

Kami quit her job as a historian when she realized there was no future in it.

Ryan found that being an electrician was shocking.

Madison wanted to be a musician, but she just wasn't noteworthy.

The nurse was nervous about giving a vaccination, but she gave it her best shot.

Mechanics never quit. They just retire.

Her decision to become a pilot was still up in the air.

The pilot who flew through a rainbow during his flight test passed with flying colors.

Pilots have a lot of friends in high places.

Animators always know where to draw the line.

The party planner was always the first to arrive because he did not want to be second guest by anyone.

Working as an elevator operator has its ups and downs.

The mechanic bolted out of his shop when he realized he was surrounded by nuts.

Marine biologists like to see a friend or sea anemone.

The nurse went to art school to learn to draw blood.

The mechanic was in pain because he wrenched his back.

A good editor can keep a reader spellbound.

Avery wanted to be a doctor, but she didn't have any patience.

The mime wanted to say something, but he wasn't aloud.

The photographer was in a hurry because he knew the event would be over in a flash.

Eric became a professional fisherman, but he couldn't live on the net income.

An electrician is a bright spark who knows what's watt.

Animators are colorful people who draw on their emotions.

Lifeguards are always getting immersed in their work.

Construction workers like to break new ground.

The optician tripped and made quite the spectacle of herself.

A weatherman broke his arms and legs. He had to call the doctor about his four casts.

The TV producer was going to prerecord a pie-eating contest, but he decided to do a live feed.

The beautician was behind on her make-up work.

The party planner wanted to use elaborate ceiling decorations, but they were over her head.

When the animator tried to draw a cube, he had a mental block.

An electric company is always looking for high-energy employees.

Event planners who arrive late to parties will find they were beaten to the punch.

The third-generation clothes designer had it in her jeans.

When the designer was asked how her dress was coming, she replied, "Sew far, sew good."

The radio host ate a lot of crunchy food so she could always get her sound bites.

The garbage man never smiled. He was always in the dumps.

HOW TO BE FUNNY

KNOCK, KNOCK!

The following tips will help you become rich, famous, and popular. Well, maybe not. However, they will help you tell a good joke.

WHAT TO DO:

- Know the joke.
- Allow suspense to build, but don't drag it out too long.
- Make the punch line clear.
- Be confident, use emotion, and smile.

WHAT NOT TO DO:

- Do not ask your friend over and over if they "get it."
- Do not speak in a different language than your audience.
- Do not tell the same joke every day.
- Do not keep saying, "This joke is so funny!"